Ms. Hall is a goofball!

Special thanks to
Tommy Gemma and Terry Sirrell

My Weirdest School #12: Ms. Hall Is a Goofball!
Text copyright © 2018 by Dan Gutman
Illustrations copyright © 2018 by Jim Paillot

978-0-06-242945-2 (pbk. bdg.)—ISBN 978-0-06-242946-9 (library bdg.)

Typography by Laura Mock
18 19 20 21 22   CG/LSCH   10 9 8 7 6 5 4 3 2 1
❖
First Edition

Ms. Hall Is a Goofball!

Dan Gutman

A
may
exce
infor

ISBN

Founta
Bolingu.
(630) 759-2

Contents

Big News!

My name is A.J. and I hate current events.

Do you know what current events are? In Mr. Cooper's class, once a week we have to bring in an article we cut out of the newspaper. Then we have to stand in front of the class and talk about it.

So the other day, we had current events, and I forgot to bring in an article.

Everybody got up and talked about their current event.

Andrea Young, this annoying girl with curly brown hair, talked about some furry animals that might go extinct.

Michael, who never ties his shoes, talked about last week's pro football games.

Ryan, who will eat anything, talked about some new food that nobody ever heard of.

Alexia, this girl who rides a skateboard all the time, talked about a new skate park that's opening up.

Neil, who we call the nude kid even though he wears clothes, talked about the Statue of Liberty. It has a poem on it that says, "Give me your tired, your poor, your huddled masses yearning to breathe free."*

I was hoping Mr. Cooper wouldn't call on me. So instead of looking at him, I looked at the floor. If you don't want the teacher to call on you, always look at the floor. That's the first rule of being a kid.

"Your turn, A.J.," said Mr. Cooper.

Bummer in the summer! I didn't know what to say. I didn't know what to do. I had to think fast.

"My dog ate my current event," I said.

"A.J.," Mr. Cooper replied, "you don't have a dog."

---

*Wow, I didn't know so many people had respiratory problems.

Oh, yeah.

"That's the third time in a row that you forgot to bring in a current event, A.J."

"Well," I told Mr. Cooper, "it doesn't make sense that we have to do current events anyway. Current events are happening right *now*, and you can't bring them in because they're too busy happening. If you ask me, they shouldn't be called current events because once they're in the newspaper, they're not current anymore. They should be called *old* events."

Mr. Cooper started rubbing his forehead with his fingers. Grown-ups do that all the time. Nobody knows why. Maybe they need a head massage.

4

Speaking of heads, you'll never believe who poked his head into the door at that moment.

Nobody! Doors are made of wood. Why would you poke your head into a piece of wood?

But you'll never believe who poked his head into the door*way*.

It was Mr. Klutz, our principal! He has no hair at all. I mean *none*. He would be taller if he had some hair on top of his head.

"Did I hear somebody say current events aren't current?" he said. "Well, I have some news, and it just happened a minute ago."

"What is it?" we all asked.

"Ms. LaGrange is leaving us."

"Noooooooooo!" we all shouted.

Ms. LaGrange is our lunch lady. She's from France, and she always says weird words like *bonjour*, whatever *that* means. She also writes secret messages in the mashed potatoes. Ms. LaGrange is strange.

When they heard that she was leaving, everybody started yelling and screaming and shrieking and hooting and hollering and freaking out.

Mr. Klutz held up his hand and made a peace sign with his fingers, which means "shut up!"

"Ms. LaGrange is going back to France,"

he told us. "She's being deported."

Nobody knew what that meant, so Little Miss I-Know-Everything looked it up on her smartphone. Deported is when they take some of those tired, poor people who can't breathe and send them back where they came from.

"Gotta run," said Mr. Klutz. "I have to go find a new lunch lady!"

Lunch Is
My Life

After all the excitement was over, Mr. Cooper told us to turn to page twenty-three in our math books. But nobody could pay attention to math. We were all sad about Ms. LaGrange. She was nice.

"How is Mr. Klutz going to find a new lunch lady?" asked Emily, who is Andrea's crybaby friend.

"He'll probably go to Rent-A-Lunch Lady," I replied. "You can rent anything."

Mr. Cooper told us to stop chatting and turn back to page twenty-three in our math books. But you'll never believe who poked his head into the door at that moment.

Nobody! It would hurt if you poked your head into a door. I thought we went over that in Chapter One.

But you'll never believe who poked his head into the door*way*.

It was Mr. Klutz *again*!

"Guess what?" he asked.

"Your butt?" I replied. Any time any-body asks what's up, you should always reply "your butt." That's the first rule of being a kid.

"I found our new lunch lady!" Mr. Klutz said excitedly.

Wow, *that* was fast!

At that moment, the weirdest thing in the history of the world happened. Some lady came roller-skating into the room. She was wearing a white uniform with an apron over it and yellow rubber gloves. Her hair looked like it was gray, but it was almost blue. And she was wearing a net over her hair, like she needed to catch some fish or something.

"Hi everybody!" the lady said. "I'm Ms. Hall!"

Mr. Klutz told us that when he went outside to look for a new lunch lady, Ms. Hall happened to be roller-skating down the street. So he hired her on the spot.

Huh! How often does *that* happen?

"I'm so excited to be your new lunch lady," Ms. Hall told us. "Lunch is my life. You know how everybody says breakfast is the most important meal of the day? Well, I think that's wrong. Breakfast is way overrated. I say *lunch* is the most important meal of the day."

Wow, she's really passionate about ranking the meals of the day.

"Welcome to Ella Mentry School, Ms. Hall," said Mr. Klutz. "What will you be making us for lunch today?"

"Veggies," she replied. "Lots of veggies!"

Oh no! Not veggies! People who eat veggies are plant eaters. I'm not going to eat plants.

"I love veggies!" shouted Andrea, who loves everything I hate.

"Me too!" shouted Emily, who loves everything Andrea loves.

"That's great!" said Ms. Hall. "Veggies are very important for good health. Did you know that obesity rates have more than tripled since the 1970s? I think the solution to the problem is to get kids eating more veggies."

"Obesity?" I asked. "What's obesity?"

"That's when beasts come to the city," said Michael.

"Stop trying to scare Emily," said Andrea.

"There are beasts in the city?" asked Emily. "I'm scared."

"Help!" hollered Neil. "The beasts are coming! Call 911!"

"Run for your lives!" yelled Ryan.

Everybody started yelling and screaming and shrieking and hooting and hollering and freaking out.

"We've got to *do* something!" shouted Emily. Then she went running out of the room.

Sheesh, get a grip! That girl will fall for anything.

Mystery Meat and Nofu

After that, we had to go to science class.

"Pringle up, everybody!" said Mr. Cooper.

We lined up in single file and walked a million hundred miles to the science room.

Our science teacher is Mr. Docker. But when we got to the science room, Mr. Docker was talking with the computer teacher, Mrs. Yonkers; the new lunch lady, Ms. Hall; and Mr. Harrison, the guy who fixes the copy machines and stuff when it breaks.

"Good morning," said Mr. Docker. "In honor of our new lunch lady, Ms. Hall, today we're going to talk about some exciting new developments in food technology. Mr. Harrison, would you like to start things off?"

Mr. Harrison went up to the front of the room. He had a little white thing in his hand, but I couldn't tell what it was.

"I've been working in my workshop on this new tool that you kids will be able to use in the lunchroom," he explained.

"What is that thing?" asked Mr. Docker.

"You know what a spork is, right?" said Mr. Harrison. "It's a spoon and a fork all in one. Well, I've developed a *new* utensil. It's a fork, knife, *and* spoon all in one."

"That's very interesting," said Mr. Docker. "What do you call it?"

"I call it a knoof," said Mr. Harrison. "Knife, spoon, and fork."

"How do you spell 'knoof'?" asked Andrea, who always cares about how words are spelled just in case they'll be on a spelling test someday. What is her problem?

"*K-N-O-O-F*," he replied. "The *K* is silent."*

---

*If the *K* is silent, why is it there? If you ask me, they should get rid of the letter *K*.

"That's a great idea!" said Ms. Hall.
"I can't wait to try out a knoof at lunch
today."

We all clapped our hands in circles to
give Mr. Harrison a round of applause.

"Okay, Ms. Hall, you have the floor," said Mr. Docker.

That was weird. What does she need the floor for? Who wants a floor anyway?

Ms. Hall held up a plate full of cupcakes. Yum!

"Thank you," she said. "I wanted to give the kids a sneak peek at my new recipe: meatball cupcakes with mashed potato icing!"

"That sounds yummy!" said Andrea.

"I agree," said Emily, who agrees with everything Andrea says.

"Gross!" I said. "What kind of meat is in a meatball cupcake?"

"Mystery meat," said Ms. Hall.

"What's mystery meat?" we all asked.

"If I told you, it wouldn't be a mystery," said Ms. Hall.

That was weird. We all clapped our hands in circles to give Ms. Hall a round of applause.

Next it was Mrs. Yonkers's turn. She picked up a few plates that were on the windowsill.

"As you know, it's important for kids to eat veggies," said Mrs. Yonkers. "So Mr.

Docker and I have been working in the lab. We came up with a few ideas."

Mr. Docker held up a box of Twinkies.

"*Now* you're talking my language!" I said. "I love Twinkies!"

"Oh, these aren't Twinkies," Mr. Docker said. "They're *Vinkies*. We took regular Twinkies, scooped out the cream filling, and put veggies in there instead. You're gonna love 'em!"

"That's a great idea!" said Ms. Hall.

Ugh, gross! Veggie-filled Twinkies? I thought I was gonna throw up.

Next Mrs. Yonkers held up a big green pepper.

"It looks like a regular pepper, right?" she said, cutting it open with a knife. "But

it's not a regular pepper. There's a little toy inside. See? We can grow the pepper right around the toy!"

"Amazing!" said Ms. Hall. "So it's sort of like a Happy Meal."

More like a Sad Meal, if you ask me.

"And *this* is our masterpiece," Mr. Docker said, holding up some white thing. "You've heard of tofu, right?"

"I love tofu!" said Andrea and a few other kids.

Ugh, gross! I'm not eating food made out of toes. Why can't a truck full of tofu fall on Andrea's head?

"For many people, tofu is an alternative to meat," said Mr. Docker. "But some people don't like tofu. That's why we've developed this new food—nofu."

Nofu?

"Yes, nofu is an alternative to tofu," explained Mrs. Yonkers. "It's tofu with no tofu in it, for people who don't like tofu."

"So it's tofu free," said Mr. Docker. "You're gonna love it!"

"I love it *already*!" said Ms. Hall.

"Not only that," continued Mrs. Yonkers. "Our sense of smell is connected to our sense of taste, so we've developed a new product that you spray on veggies to make them taste and smell like meat."

Mr. Docker took a can of something and sprayed it on a piece of nofu.

"See?" he said. "It's canned meat spray!"

"It's like portable meat in a can!" said Mrs. Yonkers.

Ms. Hall picked up the piece of nofu with

meat spray on it and took a bite.

"Mmmm!" she said. "Veggie meat! It's delicious! I *love* it!"

Portable meat spray in a can? Ugh. All that stuff sounded horrible.

And those teachers are weird.

My Name Is A.J. and I Hate Veggies

I wasn't all that excited for lunch the next day as we walked a million hundred miles to the vomitorium.* I was the line leader. Ms. Hall greeted us at the door.

"Hi dollface!" she said to me.

---

*It used to be called the cafetorium. But then some first grader threw up in there.

"Dollface?" I asked. "Why are you call-ing me dollface?"

"No reason," she said. "Hey, look! I installed an all-you-can-eat salad bar!"

"What if all I want to eat is *no* salad?" I asked. "The only bar I like is a candy bar. You should have an all-you-can-eat *candy* bar."

"Hmm," Ms. Hall replied. "What if I sprayed the salad with some portable meat?"

"No thank you," I told her. "I brought my lunch from home. Can I just have a bunch of straws? I always carry extra straws with me."

"Sure, dollface," she said. "Why do you

carry straws with you?"

"Because whenever I do something," I told her, "grown-ups are always saying that's the last straw."

I had a peanut butter and jelly sand- wich. So did Ryan, Michael, Neil, and Alexia. You *have* to eat a peanut butter and jelly sandwich for lunch every day. That's the law.

Andrea and Emily, of course, went to the all-you-can-eat salad bar.

"I love veggies," Andrea said when she came back to the table.

"Me too," said Emily.

"My favorite veggie is cauliflower," Andrea said.

"Mine too," said Emily.

Ugh. I'm not going to eat *any* kind of a flower.

"What's *your* favorite vegetable, Arlo?" asked Andrea, who calls me by my real name because she knows I don't like it.

"Twinkies," I said.

"Twinkies aren't a vegetable!" Andrea told me.

"Well, they *should* be," I replied.

We all started eating our lunches.

"I don't think I'm going to like Ms. Hall," said Alexia. "I hate veggies."

"Me too," said Michael.

"Me three," I said.

My favorite thing to do at lunch is annoy Emily.

"Hey Emily," I said. "Do you like sea-food?"

"Sure!" she said. "I *love* seafood!"

I took a bite of my peanut butter and jelly sandwich. Then I chewed it a little. Then I opened my mouth wide so Emily could look inside.

"See?" I said. "Food!"

"Ewwww, gross!" Emily said.

"Stop trying to scare Emily," Andrea told me.

"Hey, maybe Ms. Hall isn't

a *real* lunch lady," I said. "Did you ever think of that?"

"What do you mean?" asked Alexia.

"Well," I said, "maybe Ms. LaGrange wasn't *really* sent back to France. Maybe Ms. Hall kidnapped her."

"I'm scared," said Emily.

"Yeah," said Ryan. "Maybe Ms. Hall locked Ms. LaGrange up in the freezer. Stuff like that happens all the time, you know."

"We've got to *do* something!" Emily shouted. And then she went running out of the room.

Sheesh! That girl will fall for just about *anything*.

"That wasn't nice, Arlo!" Andrea told me.

"Well, she started it," I replied. "She said she liked seafood."

Actually I like seafood too. One time, Ryan and I were at his house playing video games, and we decided we were hungry for shrimp lo mein. So we decided to dig a hole to China so we could get Chinese food. We got a couple of feet down before we got tired and decided to go inside and play video games again. Ryan's mom said we worked really hard, so she took us out for shrimp lo mein.

Yum! I love Chinese food. And the best part is, you don't have to dig a hole to China to eat it.

While we were eating, Ms. Hall came over to our table. She was holding a big zucchini. It looked like a baseball bat.

"I just wanted to see how you kids were making out," she said.

"Eww, gross!" we all shouted. "We're not making out."

"I wish I could convince you to eat healthier," Ms. Hall told us. "You know, thousands of years ago, people didn't have junk food. Cavemen actually had a very healthy diet."

"And look what happened to *them*," I told her. "They all died. Maybe if those cavemen ate some Twinkies, they'd still be around today."

Why do grown-ups like veggies so much? We used to have a health teacher named Ms. Leakey. She opened up a restaurant called McLeakey's that had nothing but apples. But then she was fired when she was caught sitting in a Dumpster eating junk food.

"How about tasting zucchini, dollface?" Ms. Hall said to me. "It's delicious, and it's good for you. Here, I'll cut you a slice."

Ms. Hall started cutting the zucchini into little pieces and passing them around. Only Andrea ate some.

I don't get it. Why would a sliced zucchini taste any different than an unsliced zucchini? It's still zucchini, any way you slice it.

"No thanks," I said. "I'm sticking with junk food."

"I'll convince you, dollface," she said. "I'm really good at that. But for now, I need to go run the dishwasher."

What? A dishwasher can't run. It doesn't even have legs. And even if it did, why would you want it to run? I say dishwashers should stay in one place, like refrigerators.

We were almost finished with lunch when Emily came back to the table.

"I was thinking, Emily," said Andrea. "You and I should start the Veggie Lovers Club."

"That's a great idea!" said Emily.

"You only want to start the Veggie Lovers Club so Ms. Hall will like you," I told Andrea.

"That's not true, Arlo," said Andrea. "I'm starting the Veggie Lovers Club because I love veggies."

"Oh, yeah?" I said. "Well, if you're going to start the Veggie Lovers Club, we're going to start the Veggie *Haters* Club!"

"Yeah!" said Ryan, Michael, Neil, and Alexia. Everybody was excited. Starting a new club is fun.

"I have an idea," said Alexia. "The first thing we should do in the Veggie Haters Club is to have a boycott."

"Why?" I asked. "I'm not tired."

"All the boys have to sleep on cots?" asked Ryan.

"No, dumbheads!" said Alexia. "A boycott is when a group of people refuse to do something. Like, we can just refuse to eat veggies for the rest of our lives."

"That's a *great* idea!" said Neil. "Let's boycott veggies!"

"Yeah!" we all shouted.

Alexia should get the Nobel Prize. That's a prize they give out to people who don't have bells.

Nice Try, Ms. Hall

After school, we had the first meeting of the Veggie Haters Club in my backyard. We took a vote, and everybody decided I should be president of the club. We made Alexia vice president.

So if I dropped dead, she would be president. If Alexia and I both dropped dead, Ryan would be president. Then if

Ryan dropped dead, Michael would be president. And if Michael dropped dead, Neil would be president. And if *all* of us dropped dead, we'd form the Dead Veggie Haters Club.

"I call the first meeting of the Veggie Haters Club to order," I announced.

"Clubs always have a mission statement," said Alexia.

"How about 'We hate veggies,'" suggested Neil.

"All in favor, say aye," I said. "All opposed, say nay."*

"Aye!" everybody shouted.

That was easy. We decided that the first

---

*That makes no sense at all. Why do we have to make horse noises?

order of business for the Veggie Haters Club would be to have a protest march in the vomitorium. I got some cardboard and markers so we could make signs.

DOWN WITH PLANT EATERS, I wrote on my sign.

NO-CARROT ZONE, wrote Alexia.

SPINACH IS FOR LOSERS, wrote Michael.

BEAT BEETS, wrote Ryan.

LETTUCE NOT EAT VEGGIES, wrote Neil.

We rolled up our signs and hid them in our backpacks. I couldn't wait until lunchtime the next day, when we would march around and show everybody our signs.

When we got to the vomitorium for the big protest march, Ms. Hall was in the hallway with Dr. Brad, our school counselor. They were whispering back and forth.

"It looks like they're telling secrets," Alexia said.

"What are they saying?" I asked. "I can't read lips."

"They're probably making a secret plan to get us to eat veggies," said Michael.

"Well, we're not doing it!" I said. "Right, gang? Because we're the Veggie Haters Club!"

"That's right!" said Alexia. "We'll show *them*!"

We pulled out our signs and marched

around the vomitorium. It was cool. Some kids were cheering us. Some were booing.

I noticed the room looked different. All the veggies were at the front of the food line instead of at the end. They were in colorful bowls. And there were signs on the walls: **VEG OUT WITH VEGGIES! VEGGIES TASTE GREAT! V IS FOR "VEGGIES"!**

We sat at a table and took out our peanut butter and jelly sandwiches. Emily and Little Miss Perfect came over and sat with us as usual. They are so annoying. Ms. Hall rang a little bell to get everybody's attention.

"Today is Rainbow Day," she announced.

"Any student who eats at least three colors of veggies at the salad bar is eligible to win a prize: two tickets to DizzyLand!"

"WOW!" everybody shouted, which is "MOM" upside down. DizzyLand is an amusement park where they have like a million hundred rides, and at least half of them can make you throw up.

"I hope I win!" Andrea said as she and Emily rushed over to the salad bar.

I wasn't going to fall for that. I started eating my peanut butter and jelly sandwich. After a while, Ms. Hall came over to our table.

"How about trying a tomato, dollface?" she said, holding one up.

The tomato had a little sticker on it. There was a picture of Striker Smith on the sticker. He's a superhero from the future who travels through time and fights bad guys.

"Striker Smith is awesome!" said Ryan.

"And I bet Striker Smith loves tomatoes," said Ms. Hall.

Nice try!" I told her. "But we're the Veggie Haters Club. We don't eat veggies, ever! We don't care *what* you put on them."

But Ms. Hall wasn't giving up.

"Hey dollface, check this out," she said as she pulled something from her pocket. I thought it was going to be another veggie, but it wasn't. It was a bunch of baseball cards. Instead of having baseball players on them, they had pictures of veggies.

Ms. Hall handed me a card with a picture of broccoli on the front. I turned it over. On the back, it had a bunch of facts about broccoli. . . .

- Broccoli helps fight cancer.
- Thomas Jefferson planted broccoli in his backyard.
- The guy who made the James Bond movies was named Broccoli.

"Here," said Ms. Hall, "each of you can have a card. Collect them all. Swap them with your friends."

Those cards were cool. They almost made me want to try a bite of broccoli. *Almost.*

"No way!" I told Ms. Hall as I gave her back the card. "We're not falling for your little tricks to get us to eat veggies. Right, gang? The Veggie Haters Club stays strong!"

"That's right!" everybody shouted.

So nah-nah-nah boo-boo on Ms. Hall.

Ms. Hall Is in a Pickle

After lunch, we had recess. We were playing on the monkey bars when Ms. Hall came over and pulled me aside.

"Can you and I chew the fat for a minute?" she asked.

"Uh, okay," I said.

"I'm not trying to butter you up here,

dollface. But I know you are one smart cookie."

"Thank you, I guess," I said.

"You and your club have given me some food for thought," Ms. Hall told me. "I realize that veggies are not your cup of tea."

"No. I don't like them."

"Well, I'm going to spill the beans to you," said Ms. Hall.

"Huh?" I said, which is also "huh" spelled backward.

What beans? I didn't see any beans. What did beans have to do with anything? And why would she spill them on purpose?

"Veggies are my bread and butter," Ms. Hall explained. "I'm working for peanuts here. But I need to bring home the bacon."

What?

"So you should probably get some bacon and bring it home," I replied.

"What I'm trying to say," Ms. Hall told me, "is that I thought this job was going to be a piece of cake."

Huh? A job and cake are two completely different things.

"I mean," she continued, "I thought being the lunch lady at your school would be like taking candy from a baby."

"Why would you want to take candy

from a baby?" I asked. "That's not very nice."

"I thought it would be easy as pie," replied Ms. Hall. "I'd be able to have my cake and eat it too."

Why was she talking about cake so much? I thought she loved veggies.

"But it turned out that this has been a hard nut to crack," Ms. Hall continued. "Maybe I bit off more than I could chew."

I looked to see if she had some food in her mouth. But she wasn't chewing anything.

"I guess my eyes were bigger than my stomach," she said.

"How do you know how big your stomach is?" I asked. "It's inside your body."

"Anyway," Ms. Hall said, "now I'm in a pickle."

"You are?" I asked, looking around. I didn't see a pickle. How could anybody fit in a pickle anyway?

"My goose is cooked," said Ms. Hall.

"Then I guess you should take it out of the oven so it doesn't burn," I told her.

"I have egg on my face," said Ms. Hall.

She did not. I definitely would have noticed that. She must be a really sloppy eater.

"I guess now I'll have to eat crow," she said. It almost looked like she was going to cry.

"Maybe it will taste like chicken," I said, trying to make her feel better.

"I just can't cut the mustard here."

Who cuts mustard? Can't you just squirt it out of the bottle?

"I guess I laid an egg," she said.

What? People don't lay eggs. Chickens do.

"This will be a bitter pill to swallow," she told me. "But I guess life isn't a bowl of cherries."

Huh? What do cherries have to do with anything?

"If I can't get you and your friends to eat veggies," said Ms. Hall, "it will be back to the salt mines for me."

It must have been weird to go from working in a salt mine to being a lunch lady. That was some career change.

"But that's the way the cookie crumbles," she said.

She has cookies? I'd eat some of those.

"There's no use crying over spilled milk," she told me.

"You should call Miss Lazar, the custodian," I said. "She loves cleaning up messes."

"But I wanted you to know that I'm not a bad egg," she said. "And if I can get you and your friends to eat veggies, well, that will be icing on the cake. I'll be top banana around here. The big cheese. It will be the best thing since sliced bread."

"Uh . . . okay."

"So, I guess that's it in a nutshell," she said. "That's the whole enchilada."*

Huh? What's an enchilada?

---

*Wow, she sure uses a lot of food idioms!

57

"Well, anyway, this was a good chat," said Ms. Hall. "Thanks for listening, doll-face."

"Uh, yeah. Sure. I guess."

I had no idea what she was talking about. Ms. Hall is a goofball.

Ugh, Gross! Disgusting!

When I got to school the next day, the weirdest thing in the history of the world was going on. All the kids in my class were out on the grass talking to Ms. Hall. Even Mr. Cooper was out there. He was wearing overalls and holding some shovels and rakes.

"What's going on?" I asked. "Are we dig-ging for gold?"

"No," Ms. Hall replied. "We're planting a garden!"

WHAT?!

Ms. Hall told us to start digging and hoeing and raking the dirt so she could plant seeds for the garden. It was hard work.

"How much are we getting paid for this?" I asked, leaning on my shovel.

"Your pay is the joy that will come from growing your own food," said Ms. Hall.

Ugh. Growing food is disgusting. Why would anybody want to eat something that came out of the dirt?

"Aren't there laws against this?" said Alexia as she wiped her forehead with her sleeve.

We worked for a million hundred hours in the garden. I thought I was gonna die. That's when the weirdest thing in the history of the world happened. Suddenly the school bus pulled up to the curb.

Well, that's not the weird part. The school bus pulls up to the curb every day. The weird part was what happened next.

"Bingle boo!" hollered our bus driver, Mrs. Kormel. "Limpus kidoodle!"

That means "hello" and "have a seat." Mrs. Kormel is not normal. She invented her own language.

"Where are you taking us?" Alexia asked as we climbed on the bus.

"You're going on a field trip," she said.

"Yay!" everybody shouted.

Field trips are cool. One time, we went to a museum that had an exhibit called "The World of Poop."

"Where is the field trip?" I asked Mrs. Kormel.

"We're going to a farm," she replied.

WHAT?!

Farms are boring. All they have there are plants and animals.

We drove a million hundred miles. Ms. Hall told us that from now on, all the fruits and veggies we get for lunch will be coming from local farms. We got a tour of the farm, and Ms. Hall explained how they grow spinach, carrots, green beans, and other veggies. What a snoozefest.

At the end of the tour, Ms. Hall showed us how to milk a cow. It was gross. I can't believe milk comes out of a cow. I thought it came out of a supermarket. I'm never

going to drink milk again.

By that time, we were all getting hungry for lunch. And you'll never believe what was in the parking lot at the farm.

It was a food truck!

Food trucks are trucks that have food in them. So they have the perfect name. Food trucks are cool. Everybody knows food tastes way better when it comes from a truck.

Ms. Hall said we could order anything we wanted and that she would pay for it. I ran over to the window of the food truck so I'd be first in line.

"I'll have a hot dog," I said.

"We have tofu dogs," said the lady. "This is a *vegetarian* food truck."

WHAT?!

Me and the rest of the Veggie Haters Club sat down at a picnic table and pulled out the peanut butter and jelly sandwiches we brought from home.

"You know, Arlo," Andrea said as she walked by munching a stalk of celery.

"Peanut butter and jelly *is* vegetarian."

"It is not," I said.

"It is too," said Andrea. "It doesn't have meat in it, does it?"

Andrea smiled the smile she smiles to let everybody know that she knows something nobody else knows. She thinks she is *so* smart because she's a member of PAC. That's the Principal Advisory Committee—a group of nerds who get to boss around the principal.

Ms. Hall came over to our table. She had a knife in one hand and a big cucumber in the other.

"Hey," she said, "do you kids know what goes really well with peanut butter?

Cucumbers! They have lots of vitamins and minerals, and they're good for your skin and heart. You can slip a slice of cucumber into your sandwich and you won't even taste it."

"No thank you," I said. "We hate veggies."

"A cucumber is ninety-six percent water, dollface," said Ms. Hall, "so it's hardly like eating a veggie at all."

"You know, that cucumber doesn't look half bad," Ryan said.

"Try it, Ryan," said Ms. Hall, cutting off a slice of cucumber for him.

"Don't do it, Ryan!" I shouted.

"Just take one bite," said Ms. Hall, handing it to him. "It won't kill you."

"Stay strong, Ryan!" I yelled.

"It looks so *good*," Ryan said as he took the slice of cucumber.

"You're a founding member of the Veggie Haters Club!" Alexia hollered.

Ryan looked at me. I looked at Alexia. Alexia looked at Michael. Michael looked at Neil. Neil looked at Ryan. Ryan opened his mouth.

"I thought you were loyal!" shouted Michael.

Ryan put the cucumber slice in his mouth.

"Noooooooo!" all the members of the Veggie Haters Club screamed.

Ugh, gross! Disgusting! RYAN ATE CUCUMBER!

"Hey, this is good!" Ryan said. Then he took another bite. Then he asked for another slice. Ms. Hall smiled.

I knew Ryan would crack. He'll eat

anything. One time, he ate a piece of the seat cushion on the school bus. It was only a matter of time until he ate a veggie.

"You are officially kicked out of the Veggie Haters Club," I announced angrily. "Take your cucumber and leave!"

Look down.*

---

*Ha! Made you look down!

You Should Have Been There!

We were pretty mad at Ryan. I couldn't believe that one of my best friends and a founding member of the Veggie Haters Club would eat a veggie. I will never speak to him for the rest of my life.

The next morning, we were in Mr. Cooper's class. He told us to turn to page twenty-three in our math books when an announcement came over the loud-speaker.

"MR. COOPER'S CLASS, PLEASE REPORT TO THE CAFETORIUM."

Hmmm. That was weird. It wasn't lunchtime yet.

We walked a million hundred miles to the vomitorium. Ryan—that traitor—went to sit at a different table with some other plant eaters.

Ms. Hall rolled out on her roller skates. She was wearing a big chef's hat.

"Welcome to cooking class!" she said. "Today I'm going to show you how to roast veggies."

WHAT?!

"We don't care if they're roasted," I said. "We're not eating *any* veggies! Right, gang?"

"Right!" shouted Alexia, Michael, and Neil.

"You don't have to eat *anything*, doll-face," said Ms. Hall. "But watch this!"

She rolled over to a big table that had onions, carrots, asparagus, and other yucky veggies on it. Then the most amazing thing in the history of the world happened. Ms. Hall picked up three knives and started juggling them!

"WOW!" we all said, which is "MOM" upside down.

Ms. Hall tossed a tomato in the air and sliced it in half as it fell. That was cool. Then she started chopping up all the other veggies. She was spinning around on her roller skates, flinging veggies, and juggling knives all at the same time. The table must have had a built-in oven, because soon the veggies were sizzling and smoking.

At the end of the show, Ms. Hall flipped a bunch of carrot slices up in the air with a spatula and caught them in her chef's hat. It was amazing! You should have been there! And we got to see it live and in person.

We all clapped our hands in circles to give Ms. Hall a round of applause.

That show was really impressive. But I wasn't going to eat carrots just because Ms. Hall can flip them into her hat.

"Who wants a carrot slice?" she asked.

"Me!" shouted the plant eaters.

Ms. Hall told them to open their mouths. Then she flipped carrot slices into their mouths from across the room. Cool!

"Those carrots actually smell pretty good," Michael said.

"Don't be tempted, Michael," Alexia told him. "Remember, you belong to the Veggie Haters Club. We don't eat veggies. *Ever.*"

"Mmmmm!" said Andrea. "Roasted carrots are yummy!"

Michael reached his hand out toward a piece of roasted carrot.

"The force," he said, "is . . . very . . . powerful."

"Don't switch over to the dark side, Michael!" I yelled.

"I can't help it, man," Michael groaned. "I want to eat one."

"Noooooooooo!" I shouted, just before Michael put a piece of carrot in his mouth.

He chewed it for a few seconds, and then he swallowed it.

"I like it!" he said. "I like carrots! I'm sorry, A.J."

Ms. Hall smiled.

"You are out of the Veggie Haters Club!" I shouted at Michael. "I will never speak to you again for the rest of my life."

Look down.*

***

*Ha-ha! Made you look down again!

A Surprise Visitor

Michael and Ryan were now officially out of the Veggie Haters Club forever. After school, Neil, Alexia, and I held an emergency meeting in the playground. We put our hands together the way sports teams do before a big game.

"I solemnly swear," we all said, "we will

stick together through thick and thin. We will refuse to eat veggies no matter what."

On Monday morning, we were in Mr. Cooper's class.

"Turn to page twenty-three in your—"

He never got the chance to finish his sentence because an announcement came over the loudspeaker.

"ALL GRADES, PLEASE REPORT TO THE ALL-PURPOSE ROOM."

"Not again!" shouted Mr. Cooper.

We walked a million hundred miles to the all-purpose room, which should really have a different name because you can't ride dirt bikes in there. I sat with Neil and Alexia.

That's when the weirdest thing in the history of the world happened. Purple smoke started pouring onto the stage. The sound of drums pounded out of the speakers. Then the lights went out, and laser beams started shooting around in all different colors.

The drums got louder! The lights got brighter! And you'll never believe who jumped up onto the stage.

I'm not going to tell you.

Okay, okay, I'll tell you. It was Mr. Hynde, our old music teacher! He left our school after he appeared on *American Idol* and became a famous rapper.

"Gimme a beet!" Mr. Hynde shouted.

We all started making beatboxing sounds.

"No, not a *B-E-A-T*," shouted Mr. Hynde. "A *beet*! Gimme a *B-E-E-T*!"

Ms. Hall came running over and handed him a beet. Mr. Hynde ate it. Then he started break dancing and spinning on his head. Then he started rapping. . . .

"You say tomatoes. Well, so do I.

I'd rather eat tomatoes than apple pie.

All the teens like to eat their greens,

and my favorite one is lima beans.

I like dill and I always will.

You'll never fail if you eat kale.

I'll always finish my plate of spinach.

Black-eyed peas, if you please.

I'll take a glass of that wheat grass.

I got no stress when I eat watercress.

Only a bumpkin don't love pumpkin.

Cauliflower gives me the power.

Don't be a weenie. Just eat a zucchini.

I won't hustle. My sprouts are Brussels.

Just don't shriek when I take a leek.

I'm not joking, I'm artichoking."

Everybody was going *crazy*. Mr. Hynde was out of his mind! He started beating on Mr. Klutz's bald head like it was a bongo drum. The rest of our teachers made a line behind Mr. Hynde and started kicking their legs up like the Rockettes. Ms. Hall was roller-skating around and dancing. It was cool, and I saw it with my own eyes!

Well, it would be pretty hard to see something with somebody else's eyes.

"What a spectacle!" Neil said.

That made no sense at all. What did glasses have to do with anything?

We all stood up to give Mr. Hynde a standing ovation.

After that, Ms. Hall roller-skated around

the all-purpose room with a basket.

"Who wants a veggie?" she shouted, tossing little red tomatoes, rutabagas, and other veggies into the crowd.

"Me!" the plant eaters shouted. "I do!"

"Not me!" said me and Alexia.

I looked over at Neil. He wasn't saying anything.

"Uh . . . ," Neil finally said. "I . . . uh . . ."

"No!" I yelled at Neil. "Don't do it!"

"But watching Mr. Hynde rap makes me want a veggie!" Neil said.

"You're in the Veggie Haters Club!" Alexia shouted at him. "Doesn't that *mean* anything?"

"We took an oath, Neil!" I told him. "We swore we would be veggie haters for life!"

Ms. Hall came over and handed Neil a beet.

"Don't do it!" I shouted desperately.

Neil put the beet in his mouth.

"Noooooooooo!"

"Ummm," he said. "Yum!"

Ms. Hall smiled.

"You are banished from the Veggie Haters Club *forever*," I told Neil angrily. "I will never speak to you again for the rest of my life."

Look up.*

---

*Why did you look down? I told you to look up!

88

Pepper Poppers and Turbo Tomatoes

Now the Veggie Haters Club was just me and Alexia. Everybody else had joined the ranks of the plant eaters. This was the worst thing to happen since TV Turnoff Week.

The next day at lunch, Alexia and I sat at our own table in the corner. We were both feeling sad. I didn't even enjoy my sloppy joe.

"Carnivores!" shouted my ex-friends at the other table.

"Herbivores!" Alexia and I shouted back.

Ms. Hall had a big smile on her face as she roller-skated around the vomitorium with a big cardboard box.

"Who wants snacks?" she hollered.

"We do!" shouted all the plant eaters.

Ms. Hall was tossing out little bags of stuff. Then she got to our table.

"How about you two?" she asked. "Would you like a snack, dollface?"

"No thank you," I said politely. "I don't eat veggies."

"Oh, these aren't veggie snacks," Ms. Hall replied. "These are *junk food* snacks."

"Junk food snacks?" asked Alexia.

Ms. Hall reached into the box she had been carrying and pulled out a bag. It looked like a bag of potato chips. It said "Kale Krunchies" on it, and there was a picture of a kangaroo.

"Hmmm, those look good," Alexia said.

"Don't even *think* about it," I told her.

"That kangaroo is cute," Alexia said, "and the chips look kind of like junk food."

"They're cool ranch flavored," said Ms. Hall. "You'll love 'em!"

"It's a trick," I told Alexia. "They just made those veggies look like junk food to get us to eat them. Don't be fooled."

Ms. Hall reached into the box.

"Let's see," she said, going through the other snacks. "I've got X-Ray Carrots, Turbo Tomatoes, Broccoli Bombs, Cool Cucumbers, Pepper Poppers, Mean Green Bean Machines, Mississippi Munchies, and Zucchini Zambonis."

"Hmmm . . . ," said Alexia.

"I'll tell you what," said Ms. Hall. "I'll give each of you a dollar if you just take one bite. One *little* bite."

"That's not fair," I told Ms. Hall. "That's a bribe!"

"Yes, it is," Ms. Hall replied. "I'm so desperate that I'll bribe you kids to eat veggies."

"Oh, yeah?" I said. "Well, we wouldn't eat a veggie if you paid us a *million* dollars. Right, Alexia?"

"You'll give me a dollar if I take *one bite*?" asked Alexia.

"One little nibble," said Ms. Hall.

"I can use the dollar to buy candy," said Alexia.

"Don't do it!" I told her.

Ms. Hall took a dollar from her pocket and dangled it in front of Alexia's face.

Alexia took the bag of Cool Ranch Kale Krunchies.

She ripped it open.

Then she put a chip in her mouth.

"Noooooooooo!"

Ms. Hall smiled.

Rebel without a Cause

Well, that was that. All my friends had abandoned me. There was only *one* person left in the Veggie Haters Club.

Me.

Who needs the rest of those plant eaters anyway? Let 'em eat their veggies, I say. Nobody's gonna tell *me* what to put in my mouth.

The next morning in Mr. Cooper's class, we pledged the allegiance and did our word of the day. Then we had math. Then we had social studies.

I was starting to get hungry for lunch.

Then we had fizz ed. After that, we had reading.

"Isn't it time for lunch yet?" I asked Mr. Cooper.

"Lunch is going to be a little later today," he told me.

Then we had science. Then we had spelling.

My stomach was starting to rumble. I looked at the clock. It was after one. We usually eat at twelve o'clock.

"Can we go to lunch now?" I asked Mr. Cooper.

"Soon," he replied.

Then we had library. Then we had computer class.

It was almost two o'clock! Soon it would be time for dismissal. I was *starving*. I didn't know how long I could hold out without

food. I was starting to feel sleepy. I thought I might pass out right there at my desk.

"Lunchtime!" Mr. Cooper announced.

"Finally!" I said, grabbing my lunch box. We pringled up and walked a million hundred miles to the vomitorium. When we got there, I staggered over to a table in the corner all by myself.

"Need . . . food," I moaned. "Going . . . to . . . die."

Ms. Hall was walking around with a bowl filled with snap peas.

"Who wants veggies?" she shouted.

"I do!" all the plant eaters were yelling.

"No thanks," I said. "I have a peanut butter and jelly sandwich."

That's when the weirdest thing in the history of the world happened. I opened my lunch box.

Well, that's not the weird part. I open my lunch box every day. The weird part was what happened when I looked *inside* my lunch box.

MY PEANUT BUTTER AND JELLY SANDWICH WAS MISSING!

Noooooooo!

This was the worst thing to happen since National Poetry Month! I wanted to run away to Antarctica and go live with the penguins.

I fell off my chair and started crawling across the floor.

"Need . . . food!" I groaned. "So . . . hungry! I'm . . . starving!"

"Mmm, these snap peas are really good, A.J.," said Ryan.

"Yeah, you should try 'em," said Michael.

"Come on, doll face," said Ms. Hall. "Give peas a chance."

Then she started singing, and soon everybody in the vomitorium began singing with her.

"All we are saying . . . is give peas a chance."

Ms. Hall got down on her hands and knees, putting her face right next to mine.

"You know you want it, dollface," she whispered, holding a snap pea a few inches from my mouth. "You want it *bad*."

I was so hungry. I didn't know what to say. I didn't know what to do. I was

faced with the hardest decision of my life.
Everybody in the vomitorium was looking
at me.*

"Okay, okay!" I shouted. "You win!"

---

*Isn't this exciting? I bet you're on pins and needles. Well,
you should get off them. That must hurt.

I opened my mouth.

Ms. Hall put the snap pea in my mouth.

I chewed it.

I swallowed it.

It was totally silent in the vomitorium. Everybody was on the edge of their seats.

Well, not really. They were just sitting in the middle of them, like always. But there was electricity in the air.

Well, not exactly. If there was electricity in the air, we would all have been electro-cuted. But it was *really* exciting!

"So?" said Ms. Hall. "What do you think, dollface?"

"Not bad," I replied. "Can I have another one?"

Well, that's pretty much what happened. I guess I'm a plant eater now.

Maybe I'll speak to my old friends in the Veggie Haters Club again. Maybe Ms. Hall will stop calling me dollface. Maybe she'll stop running dishwashers and bring home the bacon instead of taking candy from babies and eating crows. Maybe Ms. LaGrange is locked up in the freezer. Maybe we'll find out what the mystery meat is. Maybe beasts will come to the city. Maybe we'll have to eat Vinkies and food made out of toes. Maybe they'll start selling peppers with toys inside them and portable meat spray in a can. Maybe Ms.

Hall will stop juggling knives and tossing carrot slices into her hat. Maybe cavemen will start eating Twinkies. Maybe Ryan and I will dig a hole to China so we can get some shrimp lo mein. Maybe all the boys will have to sleep on cots. Maybe I'll win tickets to DizzyLand. Maybe they'll let us ride dirt bikes in the all-purpose room. Maybe Ms. Hall will get out of her pickle, clean the egg off her face, and learn how to cut the mustard so she doesn't have to work in a salt mine anymore.

But it won't be easy!

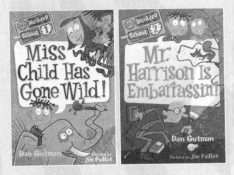